-1997-
This book
belongs to

Amber Mitchell
with Love
from Aunt Leora
on Easter

Walt Disney's
Cinderella

Adapted by Lisa Ann Marsoli

MOUSE WORKS

Once upon a time there was a beautiful little girl named Cinderella who was loved by everyone. She was sweet, kind, and gentle. She and her widowed father lived happily together. But her father worried that Cinderella needed a mother. So he married again, to a widow who had two daughters of her own.

Then Cinderella's father died, leaving his daughter with her new family. With her husband gone, Cinderella's stepmother revealed herself for who she really was: a mean and spiteful woman who was jealous of Cinderella's charm and beauty. She cared only for her daughters, Drizella and Anastasia. They were no better than their mother. They could have been pretty, but their selfish, cruel natures made them look ugly.

So the three of them put Cinderella to work as their maid and cook, ordering her about day and night. They kept her busy with sweeping, cleaning, washing, and dusting. And while they wore pretty gowns, Cinderella had only old dresses and aprons to wear.

But in her attic bedroom, Cinderella was comforted by the animal friends who came to visit her. The birds woke her in the morning with their sweetest songs. Cinderella sang to them about dreams of happiness that she hoped would come true.

Some of Cinderella's friends
were mice. She made clothes for
them, and always made sure they
had food.

One day Jaq, her favorite mouse,
rushed in, saying, "Hurry, Cinderelly!
Come-come!"

"What's the matter?" she asked.

"Visitor! Caught in trap!" Jaq told her.

Cinderella and the mice ran to the trap and found a frightened young mouse trembling inside. Cinderella freed him and then said, "We must give him a name. I've got one: Octavius. But for short, we'll call you Gus."

The mouse nodded happily when he heard his new name.

Cinderella dressed him in a little shirt and cap, and the newest member of her attic family looked right at home.

Soon it was time for Cinderella to feed the chickens. "Breakfast!" she called, scattering corn for them. The chickens came running as Bruno the dog and Major the horse watched.

When the mice heard Cinderella call, they came running, too.
Cinderella always gave them some corn to nibble.

But the mice stopped in their tracks when they saw the cat blocking their way. "That's Lucifee," Jaq told Gus. "Lucifee *mean*. But I got an idea! Somebody has to let Lucifee chase him. Then everybody else run out to yard."

The mice put their tails together to see who would be the unlucky one to have Lucifer chasing him. Jaq pulled one of the tails and it was his own!

Jaq ran out and gave Lucifer a big kick. As Lucifer chased him,
the other mice scurried past the cat toward the chicken yard.
Before Lucifer could catch him, Jaq jumped into a teeny-tiny mouse hole.

The mice rushed to pick up the corn before the chickens
could eat it all up. One chicken got very angry as it saw Gus
picking up its food. "Take it easy," Gus said to the chicken as
Cinderella shooed it away. Then he hurried around to pick up as
much corn as he could carry.

Jaq, who was still hiding in his mouse hole, saw Gus carrying his load of corn back into the house. Gus wasn't watching out for Lucifer at all.

But Lucifer was watching Gus. The cat crouched down quietly and began to sneak up on him.

Lucifer moved in close, ready to pounce. Finally Gus saw him, dropped the corn, and raced away. The cat was just about to catch him when there was a loud *BANG!*

Gus turned to see Lucifer lying dazed on the ground. Jaq had saved him by knocking the broom over onto Lucifer.

Cinderella didn't see Gus's close call. She was too busy getting the breakfast trays ready. *RRRING! RRRING!* Already, her stepmother, Drizella, and Anastasia were ringing their bells for her.

Before the bells even stopped ringing,
Cinderella was carrying the three
breakfast trays up the stairs.

But Anastasia and Drizella were
already yelling at her. "What are you doing?
What a slowpoke you are!" they cried.

"If you don't come at once," her
stepmother threatened, "you'll have
to iron my entire wardrobe!"

Poor Cinderella was used to complaints
and threats. She heard them every day.

Miles away, at the royal palace, the King was doing some complaining of his own. "It's high time my son got married and settled down," he said to his Grand Duke. "I'm not getting any younger. I want to see my grandchildren before I go." He thought for a moment, then said, "The boy's coming home today, isn't he?"

When the Grand Duke nodded, the King continued, "Well, what could be more natural than a ball to welcome him? And if all the eligible maidens in the kingdom just happen to be there, why, he's bound to show interest in one of them, isn't he?"

So that very day, as Cinderella scrubbed the floor that Lucifer had purposely dirtied, there was a loud knock at the door.

"Open in the name of the King!" called a royal messenger.

Cinderella went to the door.
"An urgent message from His
Imperial Majesty," the messenger
announced as he handed her a
sealed envelope. Then he left to
deliver the rest of the envelopes
just like it to all the other eligible
maidens in the kingdom.

Cinderella's stepmother opened the envelope and read the invitation to the ball out loud. The two stepsisters could hardly contain their excitement.

Each of them was so excited, in fact, that she could already imagine the prince falling in love with her and asking her to be his bride.

Cinderella listened with growing excitement. "Why, I can go, too!" she said.

"*You* dancing with the Prince?" Drizella shrieked with laughter.

"I can see it now," said Anastasia, imitating Cinderella. "I'd be honored, Your Highness. Would you hold my broom?" And she burst into cruel laughter.

"Well, why not?" said Cinderella. "The Royal Command says that every eligible maiden is to attend."

"So it does," said her stepmother. "I don't see why you can't go . . . *if* you get all your work done, and *if* you can find something suitable to wear."

Cinderella rushed to the attic and found an old dress that had been her mother's. "It's a little old-fashioned," she said, holding the dress up to her, "but I'll fix that."

She opened a book of dress patterns and found one she liked. But as she started to plan just how she would alter the dress, her stepsisters and stepmother called her away.

Cinderella sighed. "Oh, well, I
guess my dress will just have to wait."
    After she left, the mice took a look
at the dress pattern she'd picked.
"We can do it!" they said. "We can
help our Cinderelly!"

And with that, they transformed
the old dress into a beautiful ball
gown. The birds helped lift things
to where the mice couldn't reach.
Everyone pitched in, gathering
material from all over the house
and pinning and sewing it onto
the dress.

Gus and Jaq even managed to get a sash and some beads from Anastasia and Drizella. Lucifer saw them, but they escaped his sharp claws.

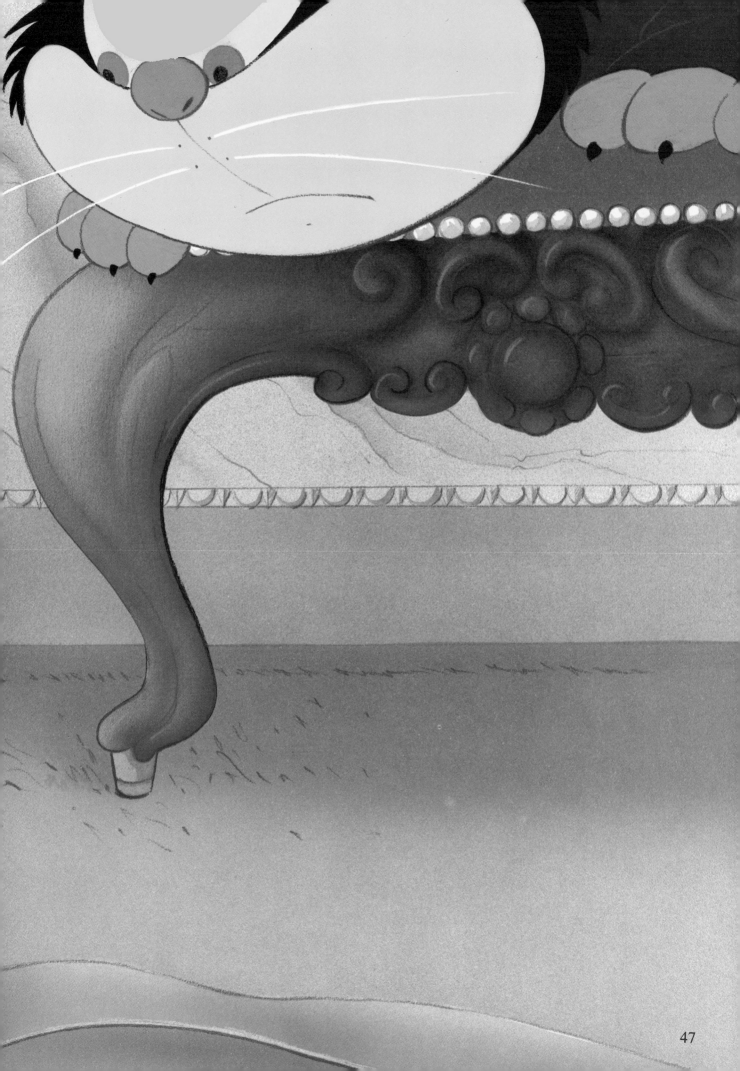

When Cinderella was at last finished with her chores and with helping Anastasia and Drizella, she looked out the window at the palace. It was too late to get ready for the ball, even if her evil stepmother would let her go. Sadly, she climbed the stairs to her room.

Suddenly the mice yelled, "Surprise!"
Cinderella turned to see the pretty
gown she would wear to the ball.

"Why, I . . . I never dreamed . . . it's such a surprise!" she said. "Oh, thank you so much!"

Then she hurried to put on the gown and reach the coach before it left with her stepfamily.

"Wait for me!" Cinderella called as she rushed down the steps.
"Do you think it will do?" she asked, touching her gown.

"How very nice," said her stepmother. "Don't you think so, girls?"

Then Anastasia and Drizella noticed the sash and other things of
theirs that the mice had used. "That's mine! Give it here!" they cried,
and tore at Cinderella's dress. Soon the beautiful ball gown was nothing
but rags.

Cinderella's animal friends watched sadly as she sobbed
in the garden. As they wondered what they could do to comfort
her, they noticed a bright, sparkling light overhead. It grew
larger and brighter, then dropped beside Cinderella — and
turned into Cinderella's fairy godmother!

Cinderella looked up in wonder.

"Now dry those tears," her fairy godmother said. "You can't go to the ball looking like that."

"Oh, but I'm not going," Cinderella told her.

"Of course you are," said her fairy godmother. "But we'll have to hurry." She waved her hand in the air and a magic wand appeared.

Cinderella and her mice friends could only stare.

"First, I'll need a pumpkin." With a wave of her wand, the fairy godmother made a pumpkin run over to where she was standing. Then it grew and its vines grew until it changed into a magical coach for Cinderella!

"Oh, it's beautiful!" said Cinderella.

"Isn't it?" asked her godmother. "Now with an elegant coach like that, we'll simply have to have . . . ah . . . mice!"

She waved her wand again, and Gus and Jaq and two of their friends turned into four white horses!

Astonished, Cinderella watched her fairy godmother change Major the horse into the coach driver and Bruno the dog into the footman. Then she turned to Cinderella. "And now for you. What a gown this will be!" With a smile, the fairy godmother changed Cinderella's torn dress into a beautiful ball gown, with glass slippers for her feet.

Cinderella was ready to leave for the palace. Before she stepped into the coach, however, her fairy godmother said, "You must understand, my dear, that on the stroke of midnight, the spell will be broken and everything will be as it was. The coach will change back into a pumpkin, the horses will become mice again, and your gown will be rags."

"Oh, I understand," said Cinderella, "but it's more than I ever hoped for."

When Cinderella reached the palace, everyone wondered who would be arriving in such a beautiful coach. "It must be royalty," they murmured. Who could have guessed that it was Cinderella, who just that afternoon had been scrubbing muddy footprints off the floor?

The ball was just beginning as Cinderella ascended the gigantic staircase. "Oh, how happy I am!" she said to herself.

The King and the Grand Duke watched from the balcony as the maidens of the kingdom were announced to the Prince. He didn't seem very interested in any of them, and even yawned.

As Anastasia and Drizella curtseyed before the Prince, the King said, "Oh, I give up! It's useless!"

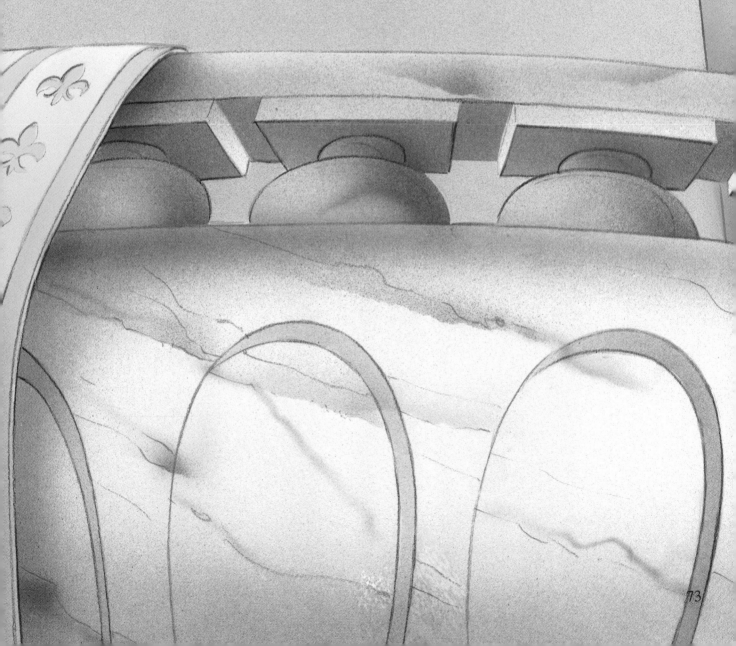

But then, as the Prince straightened up from bowing to the stepsisters, he saw Cinderella. He left her stepsisters behind and led her into the ballroom. The King commanded the band to play a waltz, and the Prince began dancing with Cinderella. Both had found true love. The King was overjoyed.

But Cinderella's stepsisters and stepmother were not. "Who is she?" they asked. No one in the crowd seemed to know.

As her stepmother watched, she said, "There's something familiar about her. . . ."

Cinderella and the Prince went out into the palace garden. They were about to kiss when the clock began to toll midnight.

"Oh, my goodness!" said Cinderella. "It's midnight!" She ran out of the palace before the Prince or the Grand Duke could stop her. As she rushed down the palace steps, she lost one of her glass slippers.

The coach dashed away from the palace, racing against the tolling of the clock. Midnight came closer and closer.

When the clock stopped tolling, Cinderella was back in her ragged gown, and her fine horses were mice again. All that remained of her magical night was one sparkling glass slipper.

The King slept right through Cinderella's disappearance. Already he was dreaming that Cinderella had married his son, and that he was playing with his first grandson.

The following morning, Cinderella was so happy that her stepmother watched her suspiciously.

Then the news came that the Grand Duke would visit every household to try to find the glass slipper's owner. Drizella and Anastasia piled Cinderella's arms high with their clothes. "Hurry with these! We have to get dressed!"

Cinderella nodded dreamily and handed the clothes back to Drizella. "Oh, yes, we must get dressed."

Suddenly her stepmother knew that Cinderella had been the one dancing with the Prince. She quietly followed Cinderella to her room and locked her in!

"Let me out!" Cinderella cried, but her stepmother put the key in her pocket and went downstairs.

Jaq and Gus saw what happened and hurried after her. They pulled the key out of the stepmother's pocket and slid down her dress with it. Struggling up the stairs with their load, they tried to reach Cinderella before it was too late.

Meanwhile, the Grand Duke and his footman were trying to squeeze the tiny slipper onto Anastasia's big foot.

As Jaq and Gus made their way toward Cinderella's door, Drizella tried on the slipper. It didn't fit her, either, no matter how she tried to squeeze her big foot into it.

Finally Jaq and Gus reached Cinderella's door and slid the key to her. As Cinderella ran down the steps, the Grand Duke said, "These are the only ladies of the household, I presume?"

"Please wait!" Cinderella called. "May I try it on?"

Her stepmother told the Grand Duke to ignore Cinderella, but he insisted on having her try the slipper. So her stepmother slyly tripped the footman. The glass slipper fell and smashed.

"Oh, no!" cried the Grand Duke. "This is terrible!"

"Perhaps if it would help . . ." Cinderella started to say.

"No. Nothing can help now," said the Grand Duke.

"But, you see, I have the other one," Cinderella said, holding up her glass slipper.

The Grand Duke quickly slipped it on her foot. It fit perfectly! He had found the Prince's true love!

Soon Cinderella and the
Prince were married. The
Grand Duke and the King
watched the wedding happily.

Cinderella's mouse friends watched,
too, dressed in their royal best.

ISBN 1-57082-017-1
10 9 8 7 6 5

And they all lived happily ever after.